MW00890159

The Cam-Mac Adventure Express

Written by Stephanie L. Brazer
Illustrated by Natalie Sorrenti

Briley & Baxter Publications | Plymouth, Massachusetts

ISBN: 978-1-954819-53-5

Book Design: Stacy A. Padula

Dedication

To my sons, Cameron and Malachy,
who have left behind a legacy of love.

And to Chris—your confidence in me
has made all the difference.

Cam set sail for an unknown adventure on a cool February afternoon while his family waved from Boston Harbor.
"We'll miss you!" they shouted as they trailed Cam's disappearing figure.
"I'll miss you, too," came the fading reply from the brand-new ship.
"Where am I going?" Cam wondered. He knew he was built to sail the high seas, but now he wished he had paid closer attention in Navigation Class.
CAM

Using only his compass and a vague memory of the maps he had studied, he travelled overnight for seven hours as the world slept. He waved to Lady Liberty, standing proudly on her pedestal. He stared in awe at the bright lights of Atlantic City and smelled the crab cakes sizzling in Maryland.
CAM

But, before he could make it to Florida, he entered what felt like a pinball machine, getting bounced around from Bermuda to the Antilles before being tossed into the Port of Miami.
CAM

"So, *that* must have been the Bermuda Triangle my captain was talking about!"

Cam was so confused and dizzy that he hardly noticed a new day had dawned. As he floated through the Port, he heard horns blaring and the sound of cheers in celebration.

"What's going on?" Cam asked a nearby tugboat named Tommy while wiping his windshield to get a better look.
"It's cruising season!" Tommy shouted over the thunderous crowd. "People from all over the world come here to pick their favorite ship to take them to any destination they choose!"
"Wow!" Cam exclaimed. "How can I get people to board my ship so I can see the world, too?"

"Well, it depends," Tommy answered. "Different people like different things like... dancing! Have you got any music on board your ship?"

Cam turned around and fiddled with some knobs and buttons, but nothing happened. He shrugged, "Nope."

"Okay, how about mountains of food? Like midnight buffets and giant burgers and all you can eat ice cream?" Tommy asked.

Cam's stomach grumbled at the mere mention of food. He peeked in his mini-fridge but only found the peanut butter and jelly sandwich his mom had packed for him.

Growing increasingly nervous, Cam stammered, “I... I... I’m not allowed to stay up until midnight.”

“Okay, okay,” Tommy reassured him. “What about water slides and an ice skating rink and a rock climbing wall?! People love adventure on board their ship!”

Cam didn't even need to look at his Lido Deck to know the builders hadn't installed any of the fun features that the cruisers would love.

"Every ship is built with a purpose. You'll figure yours out soon enough," Tommy encouraged Cam after seeing his worried expression.

Still, Cam was feeling pretty defeated. He puttered off to find a quiet place to think and became too distracted to notice an approaching ship.

"Ahoy! I've never seen you in this harbor before. Where are you from?" inquired the HMS Alannah Grace.

"Boston Harbor," Cam replied.

"Don't you mean *Bawstin Hahbah*?!" Alannah laughed.

Cam tried to laugh, but it came out as a sob.

"Oh no! I've upset you with my terrible sense of humor!" Alannah exclaimed.

"No, it's not that," Cam said. "I'm just feeling a little disappointed. I travelled all this way, and after talking to Tugboat Tommy, it turns out I have nothing to offer passengers onboard my ship. I really wanted to be part of the cruising season."

“Well, don’t get your barnacles in a bunch. We’ll find something perfect for you!” Alannah cried. “Actually, you don’t even have any barnacles, and you’re in shipshape condition. Why not be a tender boat?”

“A tender boat?” Cam asked. “What’s that?”

“It’s a special type of boat that gets passengers from the shore to bigger cruise ships that don’t fit in the harbor,” Alannah explained. “It’s the perfect job for you, and I happen to be the supervisor. You’ll start first thing tomorrow!”

ALL ABOARD

CAM

FEBRUARY

Cam loved his first day as a tender boat. He loved the feeling of all the guests climbing on board his ship, ready to have fun. He loved to impress them with his speed. He even heard a few passengers remark how spiffy he looked, and that made him blush with pride.

The days turned into weeks, the weeks turned into months, and Cam hardly noticed; he was having so much fun meeting new people every day. He especially loved the kids. Cam kept an eye out, as they would sneak off to explore his ship and find all the best hiding spots. He'd always toot his horn for an extra second or two when he would see kids pumping their arms enthusiastically in the air.

As the cruising season began to wind down, HMS Alannah Grace came to Cam with a proposition. "We've got a big job coming up, and it's going to require a lot more from you, so I hired an assistant. I put in a call to your dad, and he sent your little brother down to join you. He may look a lot like you, but he's not as fast. How long did you say it took you to get here?"

Bewildered by all this new information, Cam slowly responded, “Seven hours.”

“Well, we’re going on 9 hours now, so you’ll have to get him up to—”

Just then, a frazzled ship came speeding in, rocking every ship in his wake. Huffing and puffing, the ship said, “Sorry I’m late! That Bermuda Triangle sure is a doozy!”

Cam laughed at the memory.

"Hi, I'm Mac! Reporting for duty as the tender for the Royals of Concord!"

"AHEM!" Cam cleared his throat. "You mean *assistant tender*! Wait, did you say tender for the *Royals of Concord*?!"

"That's what I was trying to tell you," Alannah explained. "I hired Mac as an assistant so you can tender Prince Ben, Prince Gus, and Princess Mae on their trek to Alaska. They will sail with me for most of the journey, and then they'll need a strong bridge to get them back on land. But we'll have to move fast; the waters are growing colder by the day."

Cam could hardly contain his excitement. Royalty? Wait till Tugboat Tommy heard about this!

So Cam and Mac set sail for Alaska in late October, just as the weather turned cool. They took turns racing to try to keep warm and told stories about what they imagined the Royals would be like.

"I hope they're nice!" Cam exclaimed.

"I hope they're fun!" Mac cried.

They were still bantering when they reached the Gulf of Alaska.

CAM

WELCOME TO ALASKA

At that moment, a familiar ship came into view, and from it, they heard uproarious laughter and squeals of delight.

HMS Alannah Grace's voice followed behind three children. "No! Running! On! My! Deck!" she shouted at their backs. "Now come get your coats, and don't forget your penny for the bridge crossing!"

"We know, we know! Thanks, Alannah! See you in the summer!" the children exclaimed as they wriggled out of hugs.

Mac turned to Cam, "Penny? Bridge crossing? Are we getting paid in pennies for this?"

Cam shrugged as they turned their attention back to their new guests, who were scrambling on board before Mac could even toot his welcome horn.

"They are in your charge now. Show them a good time!" Alannah said. "Oh, and if they get nervous at the bridge crossing, remind them to make a wish on their penny and throw it overboard," she added before sailing off.

Cam and Mac swiftly tied a bridge in place, linking their two ships together. Princess Mae led the way, instructing her brothers to slow down and go one at a time.

Prince Ben was nearly halfway across the bridge when the wind picked up, and the waves started to rock the two ships. “Ohhh, I don’t like this!” Ben cried as he held tightly to the rope and tried to gain his footing.

Princess Mae shouted to him, “Your penny!”

Ben stopped completely, squeezed his eyes shut, and was about to throw his penny when Cam yelled, “WAIT! What if, instead of making a wish, you close your eyes and imagine your best dream world?”

Ben maintained his grasp on the bridge but kept his eyes closed. His mind wandered, and then the strangest thing happened; he wasn't on a bridge anymore. He was lying in the grass surrounded by puppies—every kind he could imagine and some he'd never seen before!

There were Labradors, pugs, golden retrievers, greyhounds, terriers, shepherds (both German and Australian!), and they were all running toward him! They played fetch and swam together, and the puppies showed off their tricks. They covered Ben in puppy kisses, and he was grinning from ear to ear when he felt a tap on his shoulder.

"It's my turn now!" squealed a hopeful Prince Gus.

Ben hesitated before relenting and moving further onto the bridge. He turned to Cam. The two watched in amazement as Gus closed *his* eyes. The sea swelled, so Gus had to hold on tight. But, instead of being afraid, he started to imagine his dream world.

The smell of ice cream and waffle cones wafted in the air. He was on a mountain of ice cream, and there was every flavor as far as the eye could see! Every hill was made of Rocky Road, and the valleys were covered in Cookies 'n Cream; the rivers flowed with Mint Chocolate Chip, and the houses were made of waffle cones.

"Mmmm!" Prince Gus got to work eating all his favorites: Caramel, Cookie Dough, and Black Raspberry, mixing in toppings like marshmallows, chocolate sauce, sprinkles, cherries, whipped cream... *and* he never felt full!

"Whoa, whoa, whoa!" broke in Princess Mae's voice. "I gotta try this!"

Gus reluctantly moved in beside Ben, and they shared a knowing glance.

Mae eagerly squeezed her eyes tightly and held on as the waves picked up.

"I wonder what she's going to imagine," Mac whispered to Cam.

As big as Princess Mae could ever dream, a bouncy castle appeared before her. “Yes!” she screamed as she ran toward it. “It worked!”

As she got closer, she realized there wasn’t just one bouncy castle; there were hundreds and thousands and millions! There was a spider-like bouncy castle and one shaped like a rocket ship. There was a big shark and a ferris wheel, a dragon, a cupcake, a ninja, and a unicorn!

Mae jumped and jumped, and she never got tired. She chuckled as she bounced on one that looked like a frog; its legs sprung out with every leap! She laughed so hard she fell over and opened her eyes to see her brothers standing over her.

"Wasn't it awesome?!" Ben asked.

"You were only standing there for a minute, but didn't it feel like an entire day?" Gus added.

Together, the three children bravely stood on the bridge as it swayed with the wind. The Royals no longer feared the swells of the vast ocean below. As the salty air whipped at their faces, they looked at each other briefly before stretching their arms back and flinging their pennies into the churning sea.

"There goes our tip!" Mac cried, causing everyone to laugh.

"Thanks for making this the least scary, funnest, most adventurous bridge crossing ever!" yelled Mae.

"Yah!" echoed Ben and Gus.

"That was really cool of you to think that up," Mac complimented Cam.

“Stick with me, and you might learn a thing or two,” Cam joked.

“What, like, maybe next time we’ll charge a quarter?” Mac retorted playfully.

The Royals were so grateful for their experience that they wanted to show their appreciation. They bestowed the highest honor upon the two ships, securing the partnership by crowning them The Cam-Mac Adventure Express, vowing to tell all their family and friends.

The Cam-Mac Adventure Express couldn't just leave the little Royals with only memories. That night, being tucked in at their new fishing lodge, the children each found an envelope on their pillows labeled, "a penny for your return, can't wait to have you back on board The Cam-Mac Adventure Express!"

By the next morning, HMS Alannah Grace's phone was ringing off the hook.

"Dogs? Ice cream? Castles? You guys were just supposed to create a bridge for safe crossing!" Alannah exclaimed to Cam and Mac. "Well, anyway, the Royals loved you. Now your calendar is booked for the rest of the year. Rest up, gentlemen. Next assignment, Ireland!"

CPSIA information can be obtained
at www.ICGtesting.com
Printed in the USA
BVHW022107050922
646256BV00004B/32